BRAVO, BUCKET HEAD!

Helen Lester   illustrated by Lynn Munsinger

 ATHENEUM BOOKS FOR YOUNG READERS
New York London Toronto Sydney New Delhi

ATHENEUM BOOKS FOR YOUNG READERS

An imprint of Simon & Schuster Children's Publishing Division
1230 Avenue of the Americas, New York, New York 10020
Text © 2022 by Helen Lester
Illustration © 2022 by Lynn Munsinger
Book design by Karyn Lee © 2022 by Simon & Schuster, Inc.
All rights reserved, including the right of reproduction in whole or in part in any form.
ATHENEUM BOOKS FOR YOUNG READERS is a registered trademark of Simon & Schuster, Inc.
Atheneum logo is a trademark of Simon & Schuster, Inc.
For information about special discounts for bulk purchases, please contact Simon & Schuster Special Sales at
1-866-506-1949 or business@simonandschuster.com.
The Simon & Schuster Speakers Bureau can bring authors to your live event.
For more information or to book an event, contact the Simon & Schuster Speakers Bureau
at 1-866-248-3049 or visit our website at www.simonspeakers.com.

The text for this book was set in Archer.
The illustrations for this book were rendered in watercolor.
Manufactured in China
0522 SCP

First Edition
2 4 6 8 10 9 7 5 3 1
Library of Congress Cataloging-in-Publication Data
Names: Lester, Helen, author. | Munsinger, Lynn, illustrator.
Title: Bravo, Bucket Head! / Helen Lester ; illustrated by Lynn Munsinger.
Description: First edition. | New York : Atheneum Books for Young Readers, [2022] | Audience: Ages 4 to 8. |
Summary: Field mouse Mousetta is so painfully shy she would rather hide under a bucket than be seen by her fellow mice,
but when foxes attack the fieldhouse Mousetta realizes she must turn her fear into fearlessness if she wants to save the others.
Identifiers: LCCN 2021028084 | ISBN 9781534493490 (hardcover) | ISBN 9781534493506 (ebook)
Subjects: CYAC: Mice—Fiction. | Bashfulness—Fiction.
Classification: LCC PZ7.L56285 Br 2022 | DDC [E]—dc23
LC record available at https://lccn.loc.gov/2021028084

To my husband, Robin, who lifted the bucket
from my head fifty-four years ago!
–H. L.

Mousetta always walked backward.

Ever since she was a wee field mouse, she had felt terribly shy, and
by walking backward, she didn't have to worry about meeting anyone.

She often hid beneath her mother's skirt. This made her mother appear to have four hind legs.

When Mousetta was with her father, she hid inside his jacket, giving him an embarrassing Big Tummy Appearance.

Most of the young mice of the field were just regular mouse children, but a few were outstanding.

They were the really popular ones.

There was Jazz, who was so cool one could feel the breeze when she strutted by.

Star looked gorgeous as she twirled her long curly whiskers and blinked a lot.

Awesome was just awesome.

Then there was Mousetta,
who never squoke a squeak.

She was . . . well, *mousey*.

During field trips (a field mouse thing) she looked for hiding places,

scurrying silently

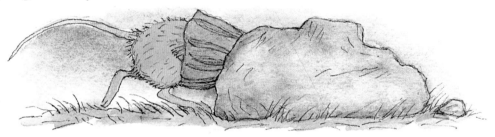

from one rock

to another.

On the playground
she buried her head
in the sandbox.

And in school plays she was
always the curtain puller.

So silent.
   So hidden.
      So mousey.

One day Mousetta saw an advertisement in the *Daily Mouse Pad*:

Mousetta stared at the advertisement.
It almost seemed to reach out to her.
Maybe to grab her.

"I can't go," whispered Mousetta. "I simply cannot."

But somehow she knew she had to.

Trembling, she put a bucket over her head for extra protection.

From what? She wasn't sure.

Then with all the courage she could muster,
she began backing . . . backing . . . backing
toward Field Mouse Field House and
Dr. Gladpaw's workshop.

Mousetta was the first to arrive.

She backed into Dr. Gladpaw.

"Welcome, Bucket Head," he boomed in a friendly manner.

Mousetta couldn't think of a reply, so she stood silently and waited, her head jangling with fear in the darkness of the bucket.

Before long she heard the unmistakable sound of backward walking.

Then bump.

"Welcome, Lampshade Head."

And then bump. "Welcome, Wastebasket Head."

Again **bump**. "Welcome, Blankey Head."

"All righty roozer!" thundered Dr. Gladpaw.
"We're all here. Let's get outgoing!"

But they never did get outgoing.
Or going.
Or even out.

For at that moment

woo oooo

the emergency siren howled
and a voice blared over the loudspeaker.

"Foxes in the area!
Run and take cover!"

Cover? Take cover? Run and take cover?

Dr. Gladpaw ran in circles.
Found a garbage bin cover.
Took it.

This left Mousetta thinking, *Oh no, not FOXES,* and standing along
with Lampshade Head, Wastebasket Head, and Blankey Head,
as if their fearful feet were frozen to the ground.

Somebody has to DO something, thought Mousetta.
We can't just stand here like frozen fox food.

From deep inside her bucket she squoke a wee squeak. "Hold paws and CHARGE."

Nobody moved.

So Mousetta squoke a little louder. "Hold paws and CHARGE!"

Still nobody moved.

So Mousetta squoke a squeak that was so loud she didn't even recognize her own voice!

"Hold paws and CHARGE!"

It sounded like a plan, so mouse to mouse, to
mouse to mouse, they held paws.
Then out of Field Mouse Field House and
into the dangerous field they charged.

 Backward.

  And right toward the menacing foxes.

Suddenly, the foxes screeched to a halt.
What on Earth were these beings charging at them?
With the weirdest heads ever seen.
And their feet on backward.

The frightened foxes screamed,
"ALIENS!"

and skeedaddled as fast
as they could.

In a moment the all-clear sounded: *okeydokeokeydokeokeydoke*

Thrilled and surprised by her own bravery, Mousetta removed her bucket and looked at her fellow chargers.

Whoa. Something about them looked awfully . . . familiar.

Could it possibly be?

But no. They were too jazzy. Such stars. So awesome.

Mousetta couldn't bear her curiosity a moment longer, so she squeaked, "Hats off."

Slowly, off came the lampshade. The wastebasket. The blankey.

And there they were. Jazz. Star. Awesome.

"You? You? You? Feel *SHY*?"

The three shuffled, kicking the dirt and wringing their paws.
If mice could blush, they would have blushed.

"Er, sometimes," mumbled Jazz.

"We just don't let anyone see it," said Star.

"We're sort of like dinner rolls. Tough on the outside
but squishy on the inside," explained Awesome.

What an awesome statement.
Mousetta smiled broadly and gave everyone a hug.

Then she saw a crowd coming their way.
"Hats on! I think there might be a celebration for us!"

Indeed, grateful mice of the field soon gathered
for a huge parade in honor of the fox stoppers.
Mousetta, feeling comfortable in her own fur, took the lead.

And this time she marched forward!